THIS BOOK BELONGS TO

Mango Allsorts
Kind and resourceful; Bambang's champion and best friend.
Rocket
Curly-tailed adventurer; full of bounce and lick.
Bambang
A hat-wearing, toe-tapping tapir; Mango's biggest fan.

George

Prepared to brush hair in an emergency.

Dr Cynthia Prickle-Posset

Untrustworthy Collector of the Unusual.

Señor Churros

Heel-stamping, hand-clapping master of flamenco.

For Andy, who knows how to dance, with love. P. F.

For Leah, daughter and dearest pal, with love. C. V.

First published 2016 by Walker Books Ltd
87 Vauxhall Walk, London SE11 5HJ

2 4 6 8 10 9 7 5 3 1

This book has been typeset in Veronan

Printed and bound in China

British Library Cataloguing in Publication Data:
a catalogue record for this book is available from the British Library

ISBN 978-1-4063-6147-6

www.walker.co.uk

Mango & BAMBANG

Tapir All at Sea

POLLY FABER
CLARA VULLIAMY

WALKER
BOOKS

Contents

BEAST

THE DAILY NEWS
BAMBANG IS A HERO!
WANTED

A Hobby for Bambang

"The problem is my feet. They don't seem to be very good at managing *fiddly* things, Mango. And my snout is too busy wanting a taste to hold on to the whisk firmly." Bambang looked sad as he came out of the Fancy Cakes and Bakes class. He also looked rather less tapir-like than usual. His normally black stripes were dusted with quite a lot of flour and icing sugar, while his white stripe, snout and ears were coated with a mixture of chocolate, butter and little sugar flowers. If only it had been a class about *becoming* a cake instead of making one.

Fancy Cakes and Bakes!

"I'm sorry, Bambang. It wasn't quite the right hobby for you. I thought you'd enjoy having something of your own to do while I practised my chess, but perhaps NOT baking after all." Mango, Bambang's very best friend, studied the list of evening classes in the busy city hall. There were all sorts available. Mango played chess in one of the rooms every Thursday evening. Bambang got a little fidgety watching her.

And that sometimes meant he got into a little trouble. There had been an incident with a water cooler only last week...

"Oh!" said Mango, looking down the list. "What about dancing, Bambang? Your legs *are* lovely – and you've got more of them than most people, too!"

"Dancing?" said Bambang. "Oh, yes! I *might* like dancing!"

There were a few different dance classes. Mango was uncertain which to choose. After cleaning Bambang up, she took him upstairs to ballet – the one she was most familiar with. "Ballet didn't suit me – my legs turned out more karate-ish – but you're a different shape."

In a bare room, with mirrors on the wall, a line of neat children in tights and leotards were holding on to a bar. Mango watched them bend their knees, sink down and push up again, in time to

music from a slightly out of tune piano. A very straight lady, with a very tight bun, was walking back and forth observing. She had a thin stick and occasionally she prodded bits of children that were sticking out in places they shouldn't be. Mango suddenly knew this wasn't going to be right for Bambang, either. She wasn't entirely certain he *had* knees, let alone which way they bent. She didn't want Bambang to get prodded.

"Actually, Bambang..." she began, but

before she could finish the straight lady spotted them and rapped her stick sharply on the floor.

"You! Child and animal! Come to the bar now, please, and begin your exercises." She was the kind of lady, with the kind of stick, who expected obedience. Mango and Bambang obeyed.

It didn't take long for both to wish they hadn't. Mango's worry that Bambang might

get prodded by the prodding stick was quite right. He got prodded a lot. Having four legs seemed to offer disappointingly few advantages. When Bambang did get one of his sets of knees to bend the right way the other set would go in the opposite direction. His legs seemed to like getting in the way of each other.

Poor Bambang got more and more droopy around the snout and ears. "Are you sure this is dancing, Mango? I thought it would be jollier."

Mango felt awful.

"Naughty toes! NAUGHTY TOES!" the lady with the bun kept shouting. Bambang looked down at his feet, baffled. A tapir's toes are splendidly grippy in mud, but not built for *pointe* work. It seemed unfair to call them naughty when they couldn't help it in the slightest.

Mango was about to suggest they give up and run away, when the prodding lady announced "Free Musical Movement time". Everyone was handed a bunch of ribbons. They could now "express themselves" as they wished.

Mango felt more hopeful; if Bambang's feet were allowed to do what they wanted, maybe they *could* both enjoy themselves.

The piano struck up a polka. The children in leotards expressed themselves by skipping around in a circle with pointed toes and high knees.

They twirled their ribbons as they skipped.

Mango danced beside Bambang with pride. Skipping apparently didn't come naturally to tapirs, so Bambang's Free Musical Movement was more of a galloping, stomping, whirling sort.

He liked the ribbons. He held them with his snout and swooped them as he went, getting faster and faster. It looked exciting.

It wasn't a very large room and a whirling tapir takes up quite a lot of space. The children found themselves pushed towards a corner. They stopped skipping. They stopped twirling. With his eyes closed and a happy smile, Bambang leapt in the air and spun. When he landed on the ground the whole floor shook. He stamped and drummed his feet, then thundered round and round in circles. He jumped again–

The piano fell silent. Bambang landed with one last giant THUMP and looked up. The straight lady had never been straighter. She looked very tall indeed.

"YOU," the lady said, pointing her prodding stick at Bambang, "must leave at once! You have the feet of a stampeding MAMMOTH. You will NEVER be a dancer!"

That was too much for Bambang. He looked at the prodding stick and ran out of the door. Mango stopped long enough to say, "He has the *beautiful* feet of a tapir, NOT a mammoth, and they're not stampeding. It's your silly dance that's all wrong!", then she ran after Bambang.

She found him curled into a ball, hiding in a cupboard full of cleaning things along the corridor. He was still clutching his ribbons.

"It's no good, Mango. No good at all," he said in a very small voice. "My feet are not chess feet, or baking feet *or* dancing feet. I think they're only take-me-home feet." Mango stroked his sad snout gently.

As they came out of the cupboard they saw a small, very elegant gentleman waiting for them. He gave a low bow to Mango. "Excuse me, señorita. I have been teaching downstairs. But we have been a little distracted by the noise coming through the ceiling. And, indeed, by the small pieces of plaster falling from the ceiling."

Mango felt protective. She drew herself up with dignity. "I'm sorry. We won't disturb your lesson again. I was trying to find the right class for my friend. But I got it wrong. Ballet is NOT right for a tapir."

"No, no! You misunderstand me, señorita! Such power, such expression, such sheer *force* is rarely found. Indeed, I have been searching for just such an artiste." He caught sight of Bambang and fixed him with a penetrating gaze. There was a short silence. Bambang looked back uncertainly. He gave a small wave with the ribbons he was still clutching.

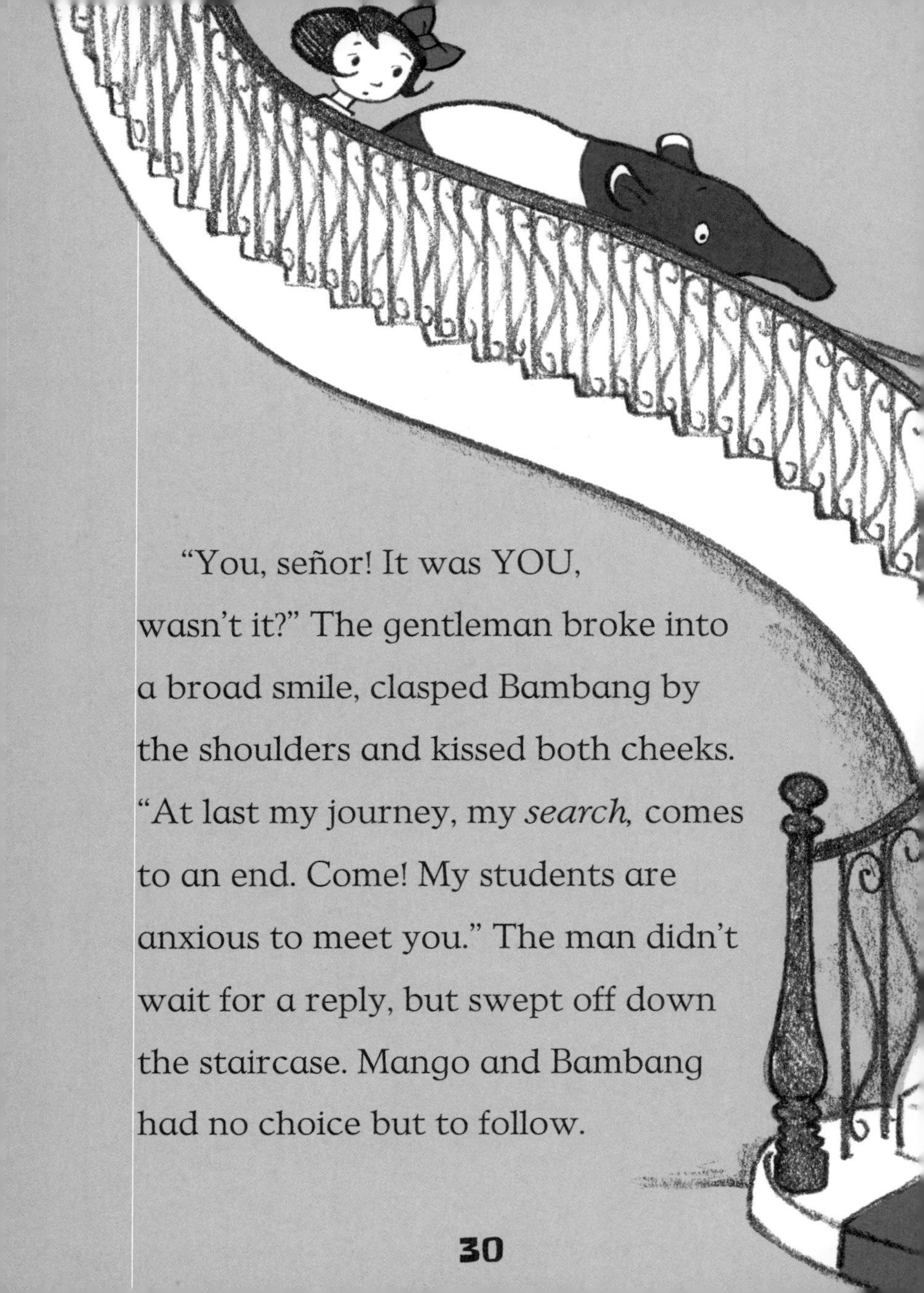

"You, señor! It was YOU, wasn't it?" The gentleman broke into a broad smile, clasped Bambang by the shoulders and kissed both cheeks. "At last my journey, my *search*, comes to an end. Come! My students are anxious to meet you." The man didn't wait for a reply, but swept off down the staircase. Mango and Bambang had no choice but to follow.

The man's students turned out to be mainly ladies. They clustered around Bambang, exclaiming and clapping their hands.

"Oh, welcome! Welcome!" they cried. "We are so happy Señor Churros could persuade you to join us. Gentleman partners are in sadly short supply."

"Can I claim you for the first dance?" asked one lady. She had a lace scarf which she threw around Bambang's neck to hook him in.

Mango could see Bambang was looking panicky. She stepped forwards and put a hand on his shoulder. She couldn't risk it going wrong again. Perhaps they should both just go home? "I'm sorry, Señor Churros, what class *is* this? What exactly do you have in mind for Bambang?"

Señor Churros looked surprised. “Why the only art that matters, of course. Here we express the most powerful dance of all–” Señor Churros turned slowly on one heel before stamping the other heel down and clapping his hands dramatically above his head.

"Not ballet – but – FLAMENCO!"

"Flamenco?" said Mango. She thought about Bambang for a moment and then nodded. "Why, yes! Flamenco. That might be just right."

"What's flamenco?" asked Bambang.

In answer Señor Churros disappeared. When he returned he was carrying an antique silk sash and a black hat. He tied the sash around Bambang's middle and gave the hat a reverent dust before placing it on Bambang's head.

“A hat?” said Bambang. “Oh, I think I shall LIKE flamenco!” Bambang was *very* fond of hats.

“It was my father’s,” said Señor Churros with another bow. “It is time it was worn again. Now,” he said, “follow me. Copy me exactly. Music, please.”

The main lights were turned down and a single bright spotlight shone on Señor Churros and Bambang. Out of the darkness came a few plaintive chords from a guitar and the murmur of castanets. Señor Churros sucked in his tummy, stuck his hands in the air and began to clap. His feet began to drum.

Bambang could neither suck in his tummy very well, nor put any hands in the air. Instead he tried to assume a proud attitude with his snout. He could drum his feet though. He could definitely drum his feet. Bambang felt the music build inside him.

At first he copied Señor Churros. Then his confidence grew and he found his own way of making feet and snout and body *and* ears move together. Man and tapir circled each other, their feet reaching a crescendo, while the other students clapped and shouted, "Olé!"

THUMP! Mango watched. She was so proud. The beat Bambang made was loud, joyful and irresistible. The whole building hummed to it. In other rooms – whether it was cakes being baked, new languages learned, car engines mended or pots thrown in clay – everyone felt the rhythm and was inspired by it. THUMP! STOMP

At sunset the classes finished and all the students left the building. Bambang walked out beside Mango with a new swagger to his bottom and a jauntiness about his snout.

"There's more to learn of course, but I think," he said, "that my feet are just right for flamenco. I think my feet are GOOD at flamenco, Mango."

"I think so, too," said Mango.

A Run in the Park

Bambang was trying to get up a tree. He was trying to join Mango and their friend George. It was a lovely day in the park and both were high in the branches, looking through George's new telescope. George, son of the Very Important Governor of the busy city, liked to spend as much time as possible up trees to escape official duties.

Mango and George were trying to help Bambang climb up. Bracing themselves against Bambang's bottom and pushing hadn't worked. Now they shouted helpful advice from above.

"Put one back foot on that sticky out bit and *heave*!"

"Wrap your whole body around the trunk and *shimmy*!"

"Hang on to that low branch with your snout, push off and *swing*!"

It seemed as if nothing would work.

Mango unwrapped a large slice of sticky ginger cake and took a bite.

"Mm-mm. Oh, sorry, Bambang," Mango called down with a slightly full-of-cake mouth. "This is too crumbly to lower. We'll save you any leftovers."

Quite suddenly, with cracking twigs and shaking leaves, a tapir appeared beside Mango.

"I did it!" said Bambang, rather surprised. He took a slice of cake. There was silence while all three of them looked at the clouds and munched.

A young couple arrived. They settled on the bench under the tree and started unwrapping their own picnic. It was very elaborate. The couple held hands and gazed soppily into each other's eyes.

Above, Mango and George made panicked eyes of their own at each other. Should they cough or say something? It already felt too late. Bambang licked stray gingery crumbs off his nose.

The young man got off the bench and produced a small box. He got down on one knee.

"Sugar-Plum," he began, "you know you're the only girl I could ever love. Will you–?"

He never finished. At that moment the reason why tapirs don't generally climb trees became clear.

The branch Bambang was on had been slowly, but unmistakeably, bending. His bottom was sinking lower and lower through the leaves. There was an ominous creaking noise.

Then a

SNAP!

and a

THUNK!

And Bambang fell right out of the tree and into the laps, picnic and held-out sparkly ring of the couple below.

"AIEEEEYA-EEE-EEEK!" screamed Sugar-Plum.

"WHAT? HOW? PIG? HO? WHOA!" exclaimed her young man.

"Oh! Ah! Oops! OW!" and "Hello!" said a rather shaken Bambang. He looked at the young man's face. There was definitely something tiger-ish about his expression. Bambang made a quick decision. He ran away.

Mango and George jumped down from what was left of the tree.

"I'm so sorry, but you really shouldn't call him a pig. And now you've frightened him. Don't you have *any* experience of tapirs?" said Mango in exasperation to the couple. "Bambang! Wait!" she called.

The young man looked down at the scattered remains of picnic and the empty box in his hand.

"I don't care what you call him, that

animal's stolen the ring! STOP! STOP THIEF!" The young man set off after Bambang. Mango and George followed behind.

Have you ever seen a tapir with a noodle salad-coated diamond ring stuck to his bottom pursued by an angry man, his almost fiancée and two children running through your local park? If you're not sure, you probably haven't. It's the kind of thing one remembers.

Once a tapir *starts* running it is difficult for it to stop.

Bambang ran through paddling pools, pigeons and pots of paint.

He ran through sandcastles, hopscotch and kite strings.

He made the sort of disturbance that gets a tapir noticed.

The busy city dog warden on duty in the park noticed. He had a long pole with a loop on the end for catching wayward animals. *And* a van with bars for putting wayward animals in once caught. Bambang didn't see the trouble lying ahead. He ran straight into the dog warden's loop.

The young man, his young lady, Mango and George caught up with Bambang just in time to see him captured. The loop tightened, Bambang was brought to a sudden, slidey stop and the diamond ring was jolted free of its sticking place.

Its owner dived forwards and caught it.

"You see," said Mango, a little out of breath, "Bambang never *stole* your ring. It just got in the way of his bottom.

Honestly. It's perfectly all right."

The man rubbed the noodles and tapir hairs off the diamond before dropping to his knee once more.

"*Will* you, my sugar-plum?" he asked.

"I will!" his sugar-plum replied. Mango, George, Bambang and the dog warden all had to look away as there was squelchy kissing. The couple wandered off arm in arm.

"Now we've sorted *them* out, perhaps you could release my friend? He had a nasty shock, that's all. He won't cause any more trouble," Mango addressed the dog warden.

"The return of sat-upon diamond rings is one thing. Damage to Park Property and Endangerment of Park Users is quite another. This animal has caused Havoc and is a Public Nuisance. He is coming with me," said the warden, unmoved. He started to load Bambang into his van.

"Oh, no. Oh, PLEASE!" said Mango.

"Mango!" called Bambang over his shoulder. It was no use.

WARDEN

"Any persons wishing to obtain the release of a Trouble-Making Animal must present themselves at the pound and make their case with all Proper Licences, or else there will be consequences for the Trouble-Maker. We open tomorrow at 8 a.m.," said the warden. He got in his van and drove away.

"But there ARE no licences for tapirs," said Mango in despair.

"Hello! Hello! Nice run. You're *nearly* as fast as me!" In the back of the van, feeling despair of his own, Bambang was comforted by its other prisoner: a tiny skinny dog with a lot of pointy ear and a *very* curly tail. She was managing to run in circles, jump up and down and lick Bambang all at once.

"Don't be sad! It's not so bad at the pound. It's warm and dry. They have biscuits! And whoever's in tonight there'll be stories and songs. I'm *often* there! My name's Rocket, because I'm supersonic speedy and one day I'm going to jump as high as the moon! What's your name? What breed are you? Are you owned or stray? I'm stray. I look after myself and go anywhere I want! I'm going to see the WORLD..."

Rocket talked and moved more than anyone Bambang had met before, but she made him feel better.

Once the dog warden had locked them up with all the other lost dogs he soon felt comfortable. The dogs told Bambang stories about the best bins for finding treats and the joys of chasing trams or exploring stinky storm drains. Bambang told the dogs about climbing up trees, falling out of them and running away. But mainly he told them about how wonderful Mango was and how she always rescued him.

"That's good, you've got someone coming for you. They don't let you stay here *two* nights," said a lurcher called Eric. "Or else..."

"Or else," agreed Rocket solemnly.

There was a moment's silence while all the dogs thought about the "or else" for those left in the pound too long.

Then they put their heads up and let out a howl together. Bambang hadn't known he *had* a howl, but Rocket helped him find it. It felt good.

When morning arrived Bambang was calm, ready to see Mango and tell her all about his night's adventure. The biscuits had been the pound's only disappointment; not what Bambang considered a biscuit at all. At 8 a.m. exactly he was ready by the door.

But Mango did not come.

All morning the dog warden came and went with his keys. Each time Bambang looked up expectantly, only for a different dog to be led away and reunited with its owner. One by one, big and small, the other dogs left.

The hours ticked by.

Finally only Bambang and Rocket were left. She chewed his ear comfortingly.

"Look," Rocket said at last, "you don't have to wait. You don't *need* an owner. Come with me! Join me on the road. We can race and jump and see the sights together! Plenty of fun for two to have."

Bambang looked at Rocket in misery. "You've been very kind and I'd love to race with you one day. But you see, I only like the city and the sights and the *world* when Mango is with me. She's not my *owner*. She's my other half of two."

Rocket touched her wet nose to Bambang's cheek. "She must be special. Oh, well. I'm sorry, I must be off now. Good luck! Don't stay here *too* long, remember … or else!" When the dog warden next opened the gate to check on them, Rocket darted through his legs and away. She really was fast.

"Goodbye! Goodbye!" she called.

"Ah, curse that dog. Gets away again every time," said the warden. "Hmm. Just the Park Hooligan left is it, then? You'd better be claimed soon. Or else..." The warden sucked in air through his teeth and shook his head at Bambang sorrowfully. "Well, I suppose I could give you one more hour."

All alone, Bambang shivered in the corner. The clock hand edged round. After the jolliness and company of the night before it was horribly quiet in the pound now. He wondered about the "or else". If Mango wasn't coming then it didn't matter *whatever* "or else" might mean.

The hour was over. The silence was broken by the solemn thud of footsteps coming towards Bambang. Coming *for* him.

"Right. That's that then. Time's up," said the warden grimly. He opened the gate...

From down the corridor came a call: "Bambang? BAMBANG? Are you there? Oh, *please*, are you still there?"

MANGO! Bambang felt a great whooshing fizziness inside. At last. He shot past the warden, even faster than Rocket, and into Mango's outstretched arms.

"Oh, Bambang, I'm very sorry it took us so long." Mango was with George. They were both dressed in their best. Even the normally sticky-out bits of George's hair were all brushed down.

"We had to get a special licence to get you out, see?" Mango unrolled a piece of parchment covered in wax seals and official stamps. It read:

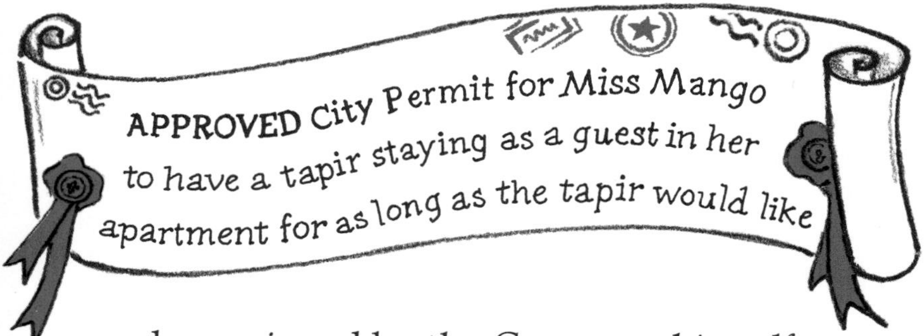

APPROVED City Permit for Miss Mango
to have a tapir staying as a guest in her
apartment for as long as the tapir would like

and was signed by the Governor himself. Bambang thought it looked magnificent.

"Borrowed the limo to take us home," said George casually. "Thought it would make us look more official. Dad's OK about it. Although I've had to promise to pass round the crisps at his next banquet *and* have a bath every day for a month."

"George, you've been *properly* Very Important and quite brilliant today. Thank you," said Mango.

In the limousine, George took off his tie and helped them all to orangeade and peanuts. Mango and the officially licensed tapir hugged each other once more.

"I KNEW you wouldn't let me become an 'or else'," said Bambang. He stuck his head out of the window and enjoyed the wind ruffling his ears.

Outside, running along the pavement quite as fast as the limousine, and also with ears flying, was a familiar shape. Her very curly tail unfurled behind her like a party streamer.

"Catch me if you can, my friend!" called Rocket. Bambang waved his snout in salute.

He thought he would definitely give Rocket a race one day. But he might not climb any more trees.

The Museum of the Unusual

The first warning had been packing cases appearing in the lobby. Strange shaped parcels marked with disturbing labels like STUFFED SLOTH – KEEP UPSIDE DOWN and POISON DARTS – HANDLE WITH GLOVES, or simply LIMBS. Then there were the thumping and dragging noises coming through the floor late into the night. One afternoon, Mango and Bambang's worst fears were confirmed when they came face to face

with their downstairs neighbour. Dr Cynthia Prickle-Posset, Collector of the Unusual, was back.

Bambang's first instinct was to run to Mango's bedroom cupboard and hide there wearing his Comforting Hat. He hadn't forgotten his last encounter with Cynthia Prickle-Posset when she'd tried to Collect him and put him in a glass case. But Mango, although uneasy herself, encouraged him to come out again.

"We can't avoid her for ever, Bambang. It's better that we just carry on as normal and are very polite if we see her. I promise I won't leave you on your own."

When they did see Cynthia Prickle-Posset next, she was carrying boxes out of the building. She *seemed* completely uninterested in Bambang.

"Out of my WAY, child," was all she said when Mango offered a tentative, "Good morning, Dr Prickle-Posset."

"Perhaps she doesn't find me Unusual any more," Bambang said to Mango that evening. Mango watched him practise a tricky swooping flamenco slide across the floor. He was wearing a feather boa, although it was causing him some ticklishness in his snout, and a sparkly fascinator.

"Perhaps," said Mango uneasily.

A few days later Mango was coming home from school when she saw Cynthia Prickle-Posset on the other side of the road. She was battling with a large stuffed alligator, trying to fit it through a doorway. The doorway belonged to a shop which had been lying empty for months. Although brown paper was covering its dirty windows, there was clearly activity going on inside. Mango could hear sawing and hammering and then the unmistakeable voice of Cynthia Prickle-Posset: "No, no, NO! This is all WRONG. Do it again the way I SHOWED you. The fingernail clippings display should be BELOW the shrunken heads."

Mango noticed a sign stuck in one corner of the window. She crossed the road to take a look, ready to run should Cynthia Prickle-Posset come out again.

Mango changed her route home from school after that. She had no desire to set foot in Cynthia Prickle-Posset's museum, even if she had been allowed. "Let's just hope it keeps her very busy and out," she said to Bambang. More and more posters appeared all over the city. The grand opening was set for Saturday.

Deep in the darkest, middlest bit of Friday night, Bambang woke suddenly. This was not unusual. Tapirs like the dark and Bambang was often up when the rest of the house was asleep. He tended to pad about quietly and rummage in cupboards. But this time something else woke him. Something that seemed like a lovely dream, but then carried on even after he'd opened his eyes. Something that was coming from just outside the apartment.

There was music; a single haunting melody played on a flute. It called to Bambang like the whistle of his long-lost mother. It was sad and beautiful tapir music that spoke to him deep inside. There was also a delicious smell wafting in from under the front door. Bambang inhaled. Fresh banana pancakes! With – Bambang sniffed again – caramel

sauce AND chocolate sprinkles! Finally there was a soft voice calling; "Free hats," the voice said. "For tonight only, and *only* tonight, ALL hats are free. ALL hats must find a home. Come and get your free hats..."

Bambang drifted to the door in a state of happy enchantment. This was going to be the best night ever. He opened the door and stepped out.

Steel bars slammed down behind him. More steel bars surrounded every other side of him, too.

There was no flute. There were no pancakes. There were definitely no hats.

Cynthia Prickle-Posset removed the wads of cotton wool from her cheeks that she'd used to soften her voice. "My PRIME exhibit. You didn't think I'd FORGOTTEN you did you, BEAST? You didn't think I wouldn't Collect YOU?"

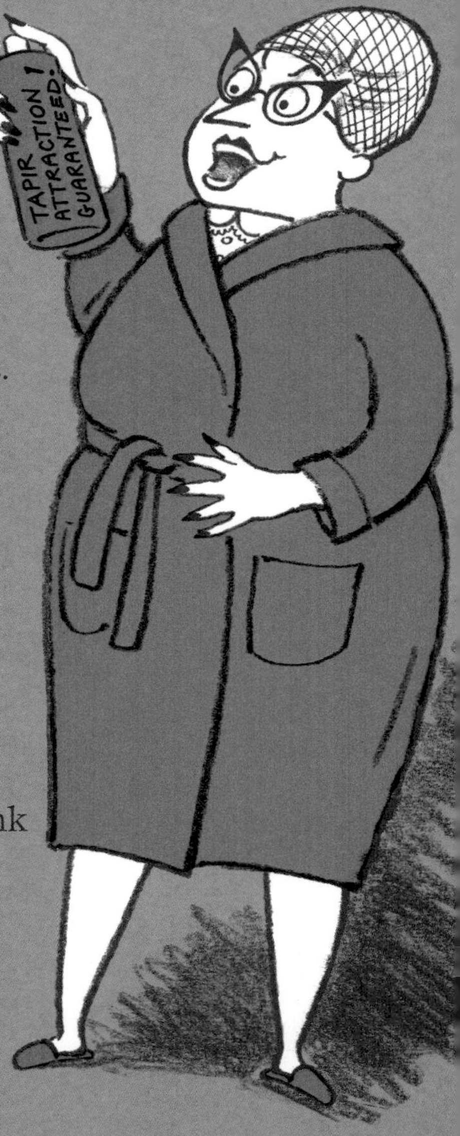

“Mang–!” Bambang began to call, but before he could do so, Cynthia Prickle-Posset held a pad in front of his snout and he fell fast asleep.

“Oh-HO! I AM an EXPERT trapper. This is my GREATEST victory,” said Cynthia Prickle-Posset and she began dragging her cage full of snoring tapir down the stairs.

Mango rolled over and dangled her hand over the edge of her bed. She liked to give Bambang's ears a stroke in the morning to wake him up.

"Shall we have honey-grilled peaches for breakfast, Bambang?" she asked. Her hand groped around blindly. It couldn't find any tapir ears to stroke. Mango sat up sharply, threw open the curtains and looked. Not only were there no ears, she couldn't see any bits of tapir at all.

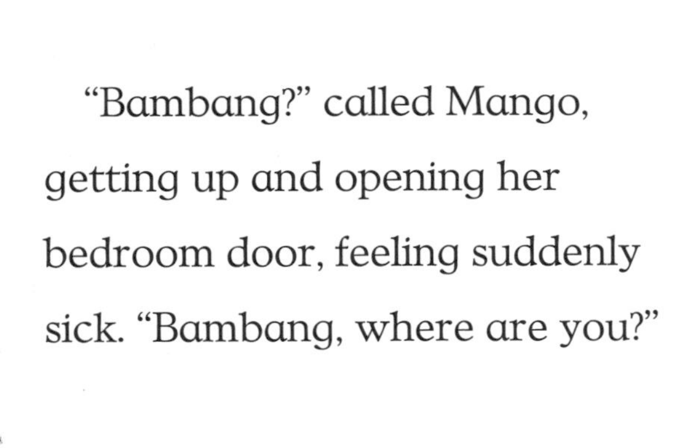

"Bambang?" called Mango, getting up and opening her bedroom door, feeling suddenly sick. "Bambang, where are you?"

Bambang was woken not by a soft ear stroke, but by a tremendous hubbub of activity. His head felt as if it was full of cold mashed potato and it took him a moment to remember the awful events of the night.

"AHA! The Beast AWAKES. My Collection is COMPLETE. OPEN the doors!" Cynthia Prickle-Posset loomed over him.

Bambang wanted to curl into a ball, go back to sleep and wake up again back next to Mango. He'd never wanted anything more. But he knew this wasn't a nightmare he could be woken from.

MUSEUM OF THE UNUSUAL
BEAST

Bambang had been put on display. He was in the window of Cynthia Prickle-Posset's museum, trapped between a selection of mummified cats and a tank of electric eels. There was no way out. A queue of eager visitors were filing in, handing over notes and coins. Some were pointing and pulling faces at Bambang.

"Stay in line. GET your MONEY ready. No TOUCHING, no PHOTOGRAPHY, no FOOD and definitely NO CHILDREN." Cynthia Prickle-Posset smiled triumphantly.

"Bambang? Oh, Bambang! What's happened? Oh, no! Oh, NO!" Mango pushed her way through the crowd, red-faced and panting. She put her hand to the window and Bambang mournfully raised his snout to touch the other side.

"Let my Bambang go, you mean HORRIBLE trickster! I don't know how you got him, but he's NOT for exhibiting. He shouldn't be here at all. Let him go! Let him GO!" Mango turned on Cynthia Prickle-Posset.

"NO LITTLE GIRLS allowed. Remove yourself. The BEAST came to me QUITE of his own accord." Cynthia Prickle-Posset retreated back inside her museum with a smirk.

The crowd of visitors surged forwards, pushing Mango to the back. Even craning up on tiptoes she could no longer see her dear friend. Mango felt desperate. Should she go home and get Bambang's licence and Papa? Find a police officer and report a case of tapir kidnap? That would involve leaving Bambang alone in front of all those staring people. Mango knew if she could only think calmly and clearly that there must be a way to get him out of that awful place. But she didn't feel calm *or* clear. And then a noise reached Mango that stopped all her thoughts.

It was the desolate howl of an abandoned tapir who'd lost sight of his Mango. Rocket would have been proud of both its length and loudness. Mango climbed on a bollard, held on to a lamppost and waved frantically at Bambang over the tops of people's heads, but he wasn't looking the right way.

The visitors in the museum and the crowd waiting outside stopped jostling and pointing and chatting, and became

very still at Bambang's howl. Then Bambang started to dance.

It was not a dance Mango had seen him perform before. It was wilder; *much* more powerful. He began to stamp his feet slowly, then faster and faster.

Even when not performed by a tapir, flamenco is an unusual dance. On the one hand it may express all of life's joy and love and happiest things, on the other its deepest heartbreak.

Bambang's dance that morning was definitely the heartbreak sort. One of his feet beat the story of running from things that want to eat you. Two others told of the terror of capture and imprisonment. And the fourth tapped its own sad song of loneliness. It was *very* emotional. Señor Churros would also have been proud.

Watching with tears in her eyes, Mango suddenly knew what to do. This wasn't about calm, clear thought and clever plans. It was about sharing a tapir's *feelings*. She started to clap and stamp her own feet in time with Bambang's. The crowd turned around to stare at her and then back at Bambang. One by one they too lifted their hands and feet and joined in.

The noise and the dance built. Inside the museum the walls and floor began to vibrate and shake. The audience didn't notice. Their claps and stamps just got louder and louder. The shaking became

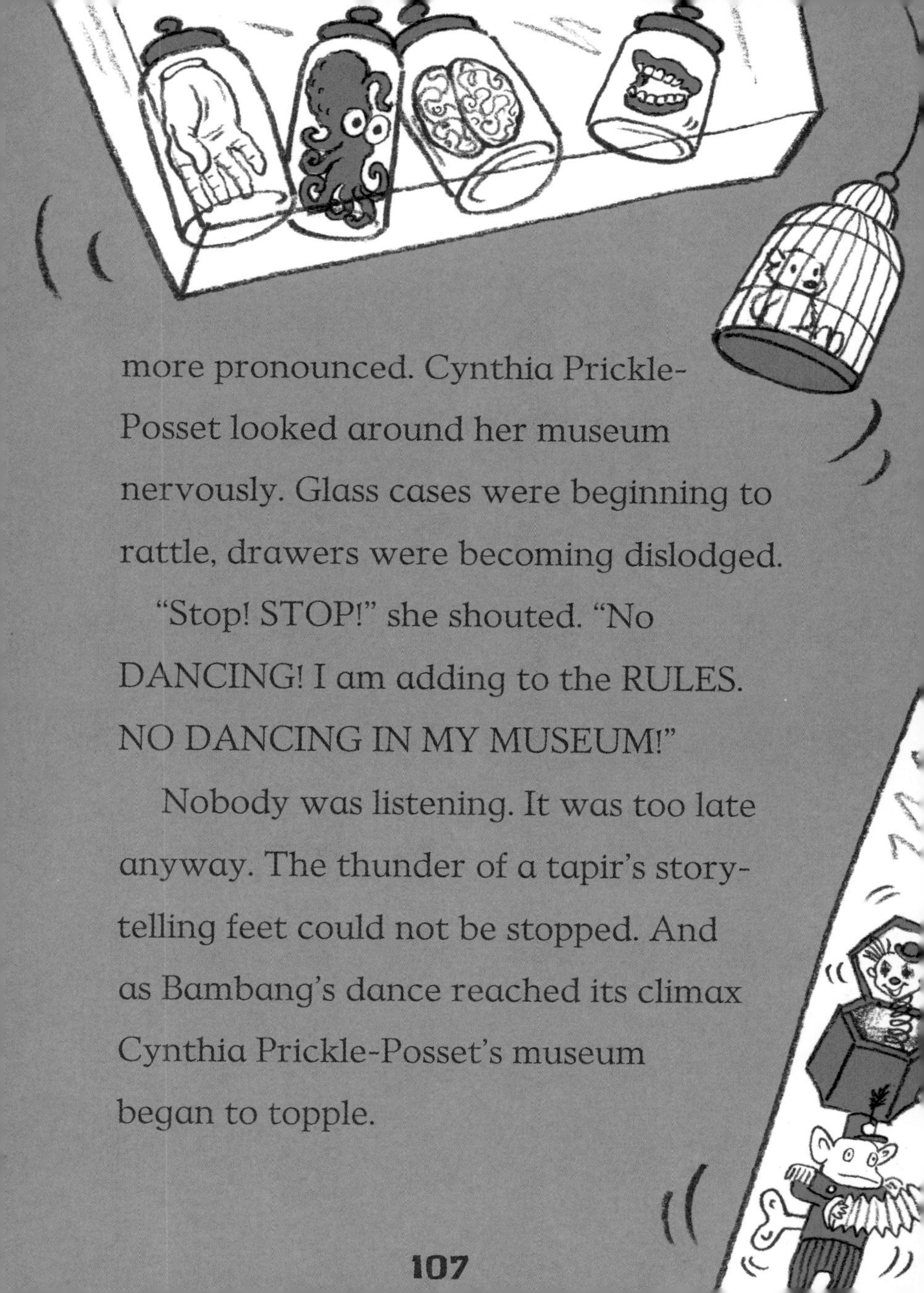

more pronounced. Cynthia Prickle-Posset looked around her museum nervously. Glass cases were beginning to rattle, drawers were becoming dislodged.

"Stop! STOP!" she shouted. "No DANCING! I am adding to the RULES. NO DANCING IN MY MUSEUM!"

Nobody was listening. It was too late anyway. The thunder of a tapir's story-telling feet could not be stopped. And as Bambang's dance reached its climax Cynthia Prickle-Posset's museum began to topple.

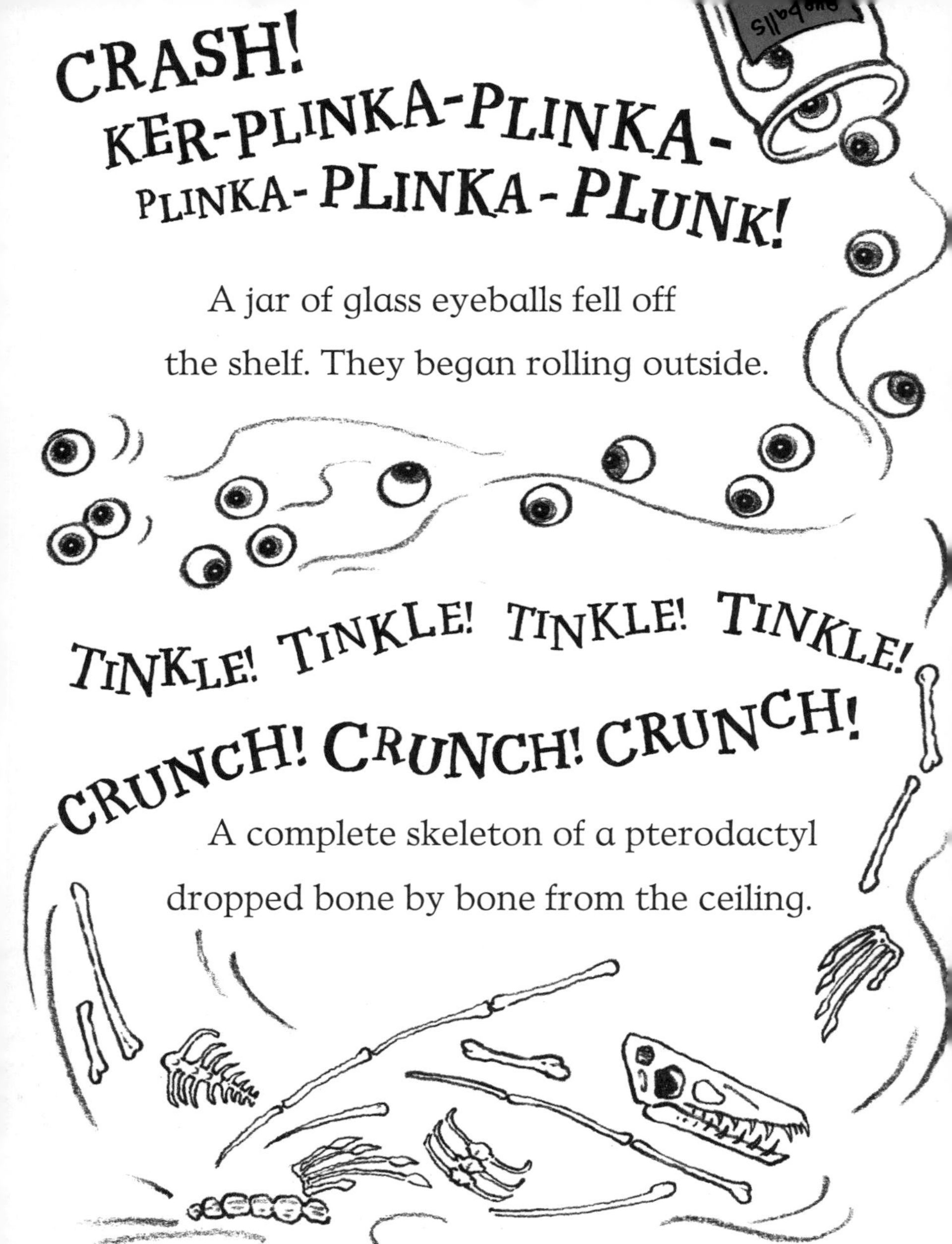

A jar of glass eyeballs fell off the shelf. They began rolling outside.

A complete skeleton of a pterodactyl dropped bone by bone from the ceiling.

A very large, very old statue of a monkey god, stolen from a lost tribe's lost temple, fell straight into the tank of electric eels.

From outside, Mango saw the chaos unfold. Visitors were running to get out, falling over and crashing into more things as they did so. More and more exhibits fell, smashed and got jumbled together. Items spilled onto the street.

"No, no, NO! My UNUSUAL things! My exceptional COLLECTION! STOP!" Cynthia Prickle-Posset was scarlet and shouting and then forced to flee herself, as objects rained down from above. She ran past Mango.

With closed eyes, Bambang kept dancing. Until a voice reached him even through his stamping.

"Bambang!"

All four feet stopped quite suddenly. He opened his eyes. The crowd had completely disappeared. *Now* he could see Mango. She climbed down and came towards him.

"Oh, Bambang. I didn't know how to rescue you, but I should have known better. Look! You rescued yourself!"

Bambang looked. The staring people had gone. Cynthia Prickle-Posset had gone, too. There was just rather a mess. Rather a mess and Mango. He jumped down and ran out to meet her.

"Did I really? Did I really escape by myself this time? Oh, Mango!"

Reunited, neither of them noticed the reporter taking their photograph.

A dancing tapir destroying a Museum of the Unusual was going to provide quite a story. But Mango and Bambang had no thought of future fame. They were only thinking of each other. And, a little, of celebratory breakfasts with real banana pancakes.

Famous Tapir

It happened so quickly. The dramatic collapse of the Museum of the Unusual and the mysterious disappearance of Cynthia Prickle-Posset were in all the newspapers. Bambang's picture was on all the front pages. Much of the Unusual Collection turned out to have been stolen or smuggled in illegally. The museum was under investigation by the police and Bambang was the dancing hero of the day. He was in demand.

Everywhere he went now people waved or took his picture. Señor Churros' flamenco class was packed and had a waiting list.

Sacks of mail *and* presents started arriving at the apartment each day. It would have been enough to turn a different sort of tapir's head.

Bambang was not that sort of tapir. Of course he wasn't. Only ... it *was* rather exciting. Suddenly everyone seemed to know who he was and want to meet him. Nobody called him a pig at ALL. He was famous.

Mango tried to be pleased for her friend. She knew he deserved all the attention.

Bambang showed her his latest fan mail when she came home from school. "Look, Mango! Today I was sent three different hats *and* a knitted snout cosy!"

"And you're wearing them all at once! They look splendid, Bambang."

But sometimes when Bambang was out dancing or invited to another party, she would play her clarinet alone and the notes that came out were not happy ones. Miserable enough in fact to bring her papa out of his study to leave her a mug of warm milk and a macaroon. "I must be brave and be happy for Bambang," she said to herself, sipping the milk. "He was never *my* tapir, after all."

And then a letter in a smart cream envelope arrived. It held an offer for Bambang.

"'Would Bambang Tapir care to perform his flamenco onboard our ship, join our ocean liner's dance troupe and travel the world?'" Mango read the letter out to Bambang in a careful voice.

"The *Queen Mirabelle* is the most luxurious ocean liner that has ever sailed. You'll get a cabin and costumes and there's an all-you-can-eat patisserie buffet. They say you are just the special sort of star they need."

"Costumes and patisserie! That sounds good," said Bambang. He wasn't concentrating very hard. He was trying to do a headstand and it was proving tricky.

"Yes," said Mango flatly. "You'd *like* to do it then, Bambang?"

"Why not?" said Bambang. His headstand wobbled and collapsed. He turned himself the right way up again. "I can do *anything* really can't I, Mango?" he added in a pleased way.

"Of *course* you can," said Mango, biting her cheeks to stop her voice wobbling. "Well I'll write and let them know. She sails next week."

The next week passed in a blur for Mango. She sent a letter to the dance troupe saying Bambang would be pleased to join them, hoping they wouldn't notice all the teary smudges. Then she kept herself as busy as she could. Mango was too distracted to play chess, but she found practising her karate helpful. She kicked and punched and kicked and punched.

"I mustn't let him know I mind. I mustn't stand in his way," she said with determination.

Bambang had to spend a lot of time in queues getting all the necessary stamps and visas for tapir travel. This was *not* a straightforward process, but finally his passport was ready.

The arrival of the *Queen Mirabelle* in the busy city port each year was always an event. She was gleaming and grand, equipped with every possible luxury. People gathered just to stare at her and see all the provisions being brought onboard and the wealthy and famous passengers getting on and off.

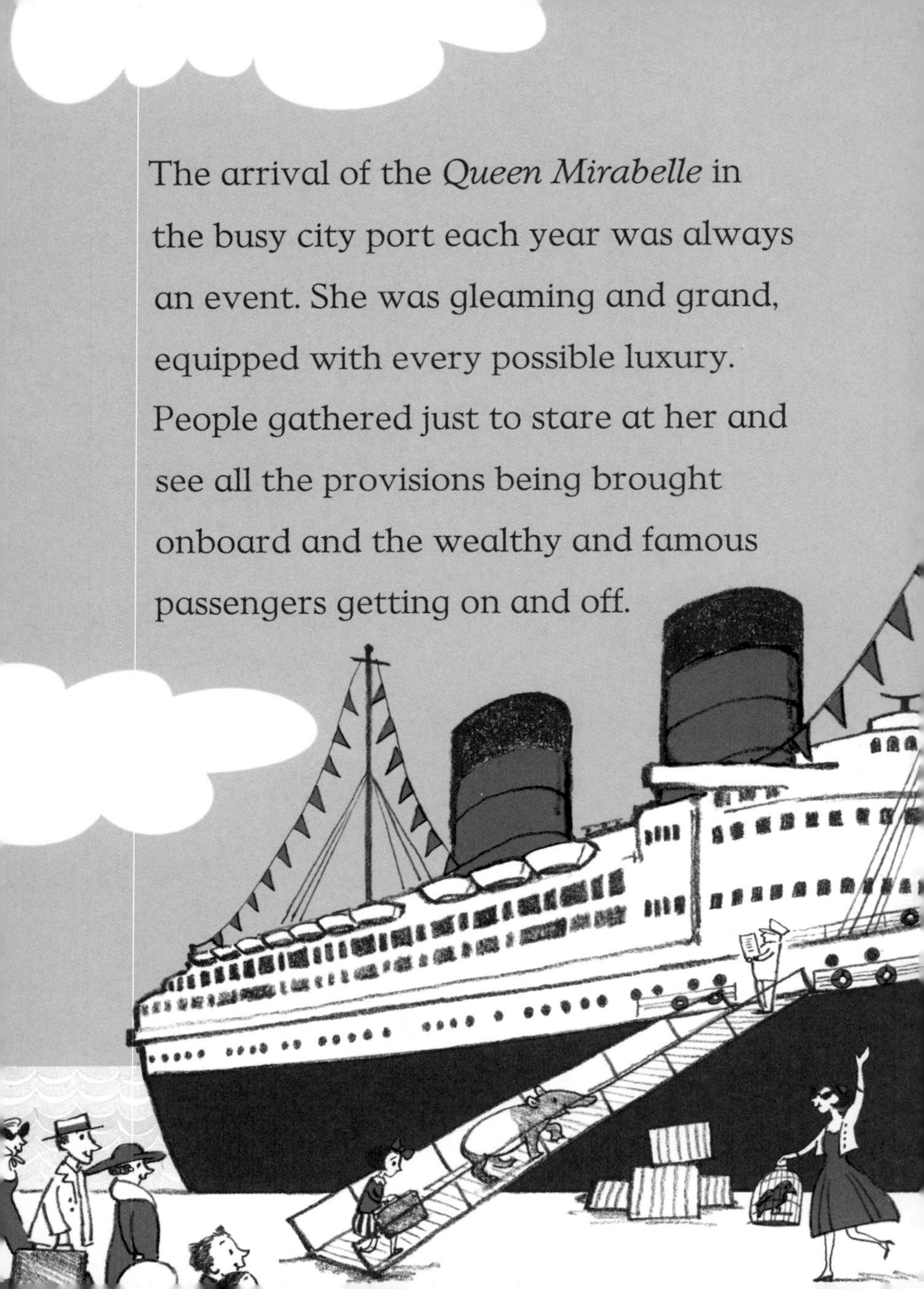

Bambang trotted up the gangplank happily, waving his snout in greeting to a porter carrying crates of oranges and a lady with a parrot in a cage. It all looked very interesting. Mango trailed behind him. They were stopped by the ship's steward at the top. He was checking things and people off on a list.

"Excuse me," said Mango. She took a deep breath. "I've brought Bambang. He's going to sail with you."

"Really?" said the steward in a snooty voice. He raised one eyebrow. "There are *no* pigs on my list."

"Oh, for the LAST time," said Mango, then gulped at that thought, "Bambang's NOT a pig. He's a tapir."

"Tapir?" said the steward. He said the word like it was a nasty thing from the

bottom of his shoe, but he looked at his list again. "Humph. Oh, yes. *That* tapir. I see. Bottom deck, cabin 423. His uniform is waiting."

"Thank you," said Mango as politely as she could under the circumstances, and she and Bambang walked forwards.

"Wait!" said the steward. "You can't stay onboard. You're not on my list are you? Move along now."

"Oh," said Mango. "Oh, no. Oh, dear. I suppose I'm not. No." She crouched down to Bambang and buried her face in the soft hollow behind his ear. Her voice was muffled and her eyes were hidden that way. The steward stood over them and drummed his fingers on the clipboard impatiently.

"Well, goodbye dear Bambang. Goodbye. I know you're going to be so happy here. I'm so proud. But come and visit us again one day, won't you? It's been..." Mango found she could not complete her sentence. She stood up suddenly and walked briskly down the gangplank. She knew she could not risk *looking* back but she gave a small backwards wave.

Bambang sat frozen. What was happening? Where was Mango going? Why was she leaving him? An awful icy realization crept over him, as he watched her lovely familiar back disappear into the crowds. His snout trembled. He was going on this ship *alone*? WITHOUT Mango? Oh, no! Oh, no, no, NO! *That* hadn't been the plan at all. How could she have thought he would go *anywhere* without her?

He leapt up to run after her, to explain his awful, awful mistake, but the steward put a hand on his shoulder.

"You get below deck now. We'll be sailing shortly." It was true. The gangplank was being lifted up. The engines of the great liner were beginning to thrum. Bambang had no choice but to go into the ship and away from Mango.

Bambang huddled in his cabin wearing his official *Queen Mirabelle* crew hat and badge. There wasn't really space to huddle as it had not been designed with tapirs in mind. Bambang realized that when he needed to leave, he would have to back out bottom first. What a silly, silly tapir he had been. Of *course* Mango couldn't come too. She couldn't leave her school and her papa! And he'd been so puffed up and thoughtless he'd let her think dancing and fame and ... and *nonsense*

mattered more to him than her.

It was a calamity.

He pressed the side of his face to the very small porthole and peered out. The ship had left port a short time ago, but the busy city skyline remained in sight. Bambang watched as the buildings and places he'd visited with Mango got smaller. He felt homesick in a way he never had for the jungle.

Mysteriously the view suddenly disappeared. Then reappeared.

Then disappeared. Then reappeared. Something was just outside Bambang's porthole and was jumping up and banging on the glass with its nose. Something was a somebody; a somebody Bambang knew...

It was Rocket!

"Hello! Hello! Hello! Let me in! Let me in! Let me in!" Rocket had been hiding in one of the lifeboats attached to the side of the ship. Bambang got over his surprise and pushed open the

porthole quickly. On her next jump Rocket squeezed through and inside.

The cabin seemed even smaller when it was full of jump and wriggle and curly tail, but Bambang didn't mind. For just a moment he forgot about the dreadfulness of leaving Mango.

"You coming to see the world after all? Fancy that!" said Rocket. "What larks we'll have. I've stowed away, but I've already sniffed out where they store the sausages! We're on our way my friend!"

Then Bambang remembered all the dreadfulness all at once. He burst into tears. He didn't *want* to be on his way. Not a bit.

"Oh, no! What's wrong? What's up? What's happened?" Rocket licked away his tears as Bambang explained about the silly muddle he'd made.

"I didn't listen, didn't understand, but it's too late now," he finished sadly. "The ship has sailed. And I've got to dance.

Though I don't think I'll ever feel like dancing again."

For once Rocket stood completely still and cocked her head on one side in a considering sort of way. "It's not too late. Can you swim?" she said.

Bambang sat up suddenly. "Yes," he said. "I'm a very good swimmer. Oh, YES." He looked out of the porthole again. The city skyline was still in sight, but only just. It was tiny.

"Then off you go! I'll pretend I'm you. I can't dance, but I can do tricks. Look! They'll love me! And I fit much better in this cabin than you do. Come on. Give me your hat and badge and jump!"

Nobody saw a tapir and a dog hug goodbye on the back deck of the smartest ocean liner of them all. Nobody heard them wish each other luck and promise to meet again one day. So nobody shouted "Tapir overboard!" when Bambang jumped off the liner and into the wide cold ocean.

Bambang was an excellent swimmer, but he hadn't realized how far out the ship had got. Or how bouncy the waves were. It was exhausting. He tried not to think about all the water around him and what other things might be swimming in it. He tried not to remember the TV programme he and Mango had once watched about tiger sharks.

Instead Bambang thought about Mango. Maybe she wouldn't WANT him back now he'd been such a silly? He still needed to explain, to tell her *properly* how he felt. And if she didn't want him around any more, he'd go back to a quiet life in the jungle. A life without hats or dancing or adventures, but plenty of time to remember happier days. Bambang put his snout down and swam with more determination. The city was getting closer now.

As it got nearer Bambang could see the shadow of the port. His eyesight was not strong, but he could see the jetty the ship had sailed from. It looked quiet and empty now. He got closer still. His heart started to beat a little faster.

There was a small shadow. A shadow sitting on the end of the jetty with dangling legs and shoulders slumped. A shadow that even in silhouette seemed to ache with loneliness. Bambang strained and strained his eyes and swam harder. Could it be? He didn't deserve it.

The shadow suddenly stiffened. The shoulders lifted. The legs stopped dangling as the shadow scrambled to its feet. To *her* feet.

It was!

It really was. It was Mango and she'd spotted her tapir, her Bambang swimming back to her once more. She ran to greet him at the water's edge.

Exactly what each said to the other, how each clung to the other, does not need to be told. We can all imagine what we'd say to our dearest friend under such circumstances. There were apologies and explanations and relieved laughter, but mainly hugs.

"Being famous is just a lot of big phooey," said Bambang firmly, later. "I'm going to lead a *very* quiet life from now on with you, dearest Mango."

Mango smiled. She had a feeling that might not be entirely true; life with Bambang would *never* be quiet. But who cared?

And Mango and Bambang went back home. Together.

Also in the
MANGO & BAMBANG series
POLLY FABER
Mango
&
BAMBANG
The Not-a-Pig
CLARA VULLIAMY
The Not-a-Pig